Football Crazy

Written by:
Gordon McCracken

Illustrated by:
Graeme Hewitson

Christian Year Publications

ISBN-13: 978 1 872734 54 5

Typeset by John Ritchie Ltd., Kilmarnock
Printed by CCB

I'm football crazy, I'm football mad!
I go to every home game with my
brother and my dad.

I love my local football team
- they simply are the best;
Although they sometimes
lose a game, they're better
than the rest.

Great grandad was the first one to devote his life in full And every generation since, for that's a family rule.

If anyone should dare suggest that football was not king, They'd face the wrath of grandad and the frown that it would bring.

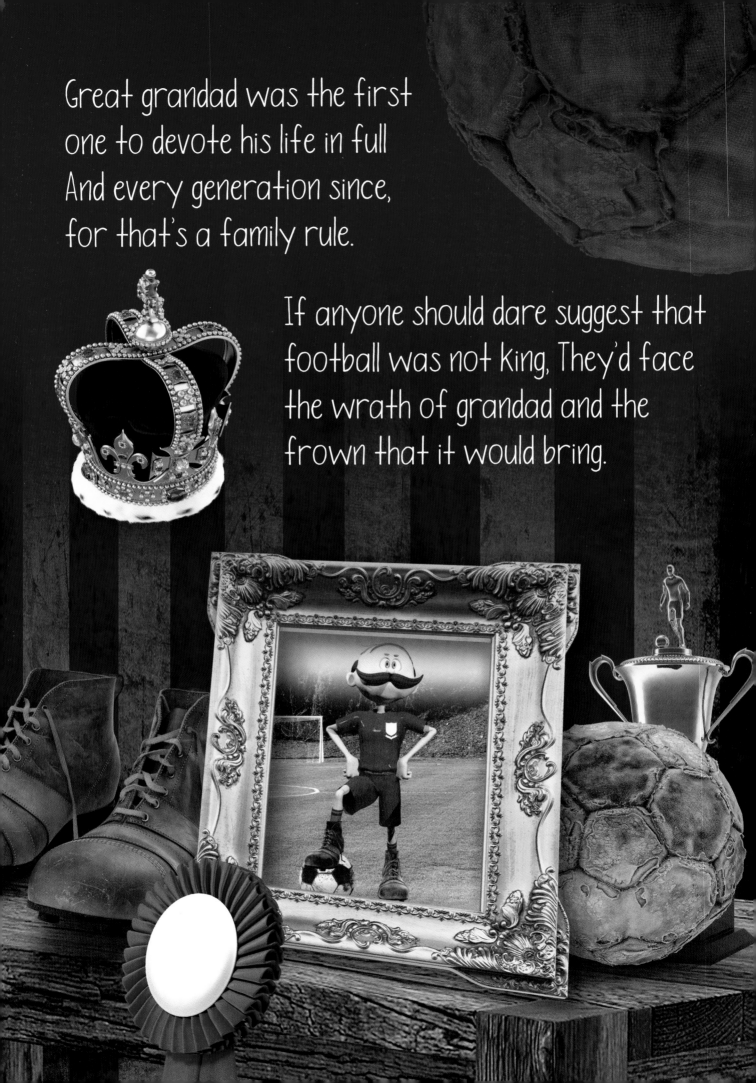

So week by week we watched them play, till grandad could not go. Now sadly he has passed away with nothing left to show.

I wonder, is it worth it all to give my heart and soul? But as I'm thinking these deep thoughts they go and score a goal.

There is no greater feeling when they shoot and when they score! I've got the whole team's picture pinned up on my bedroom door.

The captain's our best player,
and every time he plays,
I chant his name across the
pitch and sing a song of praise!

But when he missed a penalty,
the fans began to boo,
The coach brought on a substitute,
and in the end we drew.

I thought that our new
keeper was as strong
as he was brave,
But sadly he was
useless and he couldn't
make a save.

The striker, our top scorer,
he will very rarely miss;
To show his love and loyalty
he gives his badge a kiss.

But now he's being transferred, for he's got a better deal.
I couldn't understand it, 'cos I thought his love was real.

At school I got in trouble when caught fighting with my chum, So now I'm heading home to get my punishment from mum.

I hope she will believe me, that it was my friend to blame And not give me the punishment to miss the next home game.

To my horror I was grounded, and received a touchline ban. Would the team's performance suffer if they lacked their biggest fan?

But they won the game,
no problem, and without
my helping hand;
It just didn't seem to
matter that I wasn't in
the stand!

Their programme
made no mention
of my name, not
being there;
The players didn't
notice, no, they
didn't seem to care.

My mum forced me to go to church, instead of to the game. And I began to learn of God and how that Jesus came.

I learned that He had never sinned (which means He never missed), That He had come to earth for me, and knows that I exist.

For God so greatly loved the world His only Son He gave;
When someone puts their trust in Him He'll always make the save,

For He became my substitute by dying in my place
That I might know God's love and have salvation by His grace.

So now I sing the praise of One who hung upon the tree. Not one of my team's players would have ever died for me.

I know He'll never leave me, and He will not let me down – Although I'll never win the cup, one day I'll get a crown!